My Little Book of

Whitetails

By Hope Irvin Marston
Illustrated by Maria Magdalena Brown

Windward Publishing

AN IMPRINT OF FINNEY COMPANY
www.finney-hobar.com

One morning in May two newborn fawns wobbled on their long, thin legs in a secret spot in the forest.

Their mother scrubbed their bodies with her rough tongue. She licked them so hard they tumbled to the ground.

Then she lay down to nurse them.

While the twins filled their tummies, their mother washed them again.

sWIsh!   sWIsh!   sWIsh!

She was washing away their newborn smells to help keep them safe.

She led her babies to separate beds in the soft grass. Then she slipped away leaving them to rest.

The white spots on their coats helped them stay hidden until she came back.

The fawns spent their spring days sleeping in their hiding place. Their mother always returned to nurse and groom them.

She pressed her nose against their backs to teach them to lie down and stay quiet.

Her babies tucked their long legs under their bodies. They flattened their chins to the ground.

One afternoon a swallowtail butterfly landed on a bush near the fawns. Very slowly it opened and closed its wings.

Open Close

Open Close

Open Close

The fawns watched the
butterfly, but they did not move.

Their eyelids grew heavy,
and they fell asleep.

When the doe returned, the
fawns bounded to her and touched
her nose. They wagged their tails
wildly.

One baby tried to follow her. She chased it back, but it tried again. She put her foot on it and gently pushed it to the ground. This time it stayed when she disappeared into the meadow nearby.

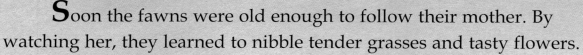

Soon the fawns were old enough to follow their mother. By watching her, they learned to nibble tender grasses and tasty flowers.

One day while they were munching leaves along the stream, they heard a new sound.

S**NAP**!

Something had stepped on a dry branch.

Suddenly, a young bobcat
was leaping toward them.

"BAAA**! B**AAA**!"**
the fawns bleated.

The doe ran to them and
chased the bobcat away.

As they grew stronger, the frisky little fawns ran and jumped through the grass. They butted each other. They chased butterflies and grasshoppers. Sometimes they ran in circles around their mother.

They were learning to behave like deer.

Late one summer afternoon
one fawn wandered off.

"MEw!
    mEW!
        MEw!"

its mother cried. She dashed about looking for her baby.

A loud **BLEA**т sent her racing toward the meadow. A coyote was creeping toward the little fawn. The fawn's mother struck it with her sharp hooves and chased it away.

One morning the deer family was feeding on clover in the meadow when the mother heard something moving nearby. She pricked up her ears, snorted, and bobbed her head.

THUMP! THUMP!

She struck the ground with her front foot to warn her babies. Then she bounded away with her white tail straight up!

The fawns followed her tail into the safety of the woods.

Autumn arrived, and the fawns' red-brown coats turned to blue-gray.

The deer stuffed themselves with acorns, beechnuts, soybeans, and field corn.

While they ate, their mother stood guard, watching and listening.

She sniffed the air, but there was no scent of danger.

One day several bucks began to follow the doe.
When the time was right, she mated with a strong one that
had eight points on his antlers.

After mating, she spent her time searching for food to give herself energy for the long winter months. She gobbled up everything she could find to eat. She digested it later when she lay down to chew her cud.

Later that day the fawns found an old orchard and feasted on the apples that had fallen to the ground. Their mother reared up on her hind legs to reach the apples still hanging on the trees.

When the apples were gone, the deer chewed on oak leaves, dry grasses, and woody vines.

With the coming of winter, the doe and her fawns banded together with dozens of other deer. They found a sheltered spot on the sunny slope of a mountain.

Before the snows piled high, they made
trails to places where they could find food.
Their furry winter coats kept them warm.

Late winter travel
was hard for the deer.
They sank into the deep
snow. Or they slipped on
the hard crust.

They stretched their necks to eat oak leaves still hanging on the branches. Finally they ate the bark.

On warmer days, the fawns frolicked in the sun.

Winter slowly melted into spring. Two fuzzy "bumps" stuck out on the young buck's head where his antlers would grow.

One morning in May the mother chased both the yearlings away. They were big enough to take care of themselves.

A few days later a new fawn was born. Its mother scrubbed it with her rough tongue and lay down to nurse it.

DEDICATIONS:

For Arthur
— H.I.M.

For Jeff, Lisa, Mike, and Danielle
— M.M.B.

Windward Publishing
3943 Meadowbrook Road
Minneapolis, MN 55426-4505
An Imprint Of Finney Company
www.finney-hobar.com

Printed in the United States of America